Slim Goodbody's
Inside Guide to Pets

RABBITS

By Slim Goodbody

Illustrations: Ben McGinnis

Consultant: Kate Bergen Pierce,
Doctor of Veterinary Medicine

Gareth Stevens
Publishing

Dedication: To Cottontail and Sophia Olton-Weber, the girl who loved him dearly

Please visit our web site at: www.garethstevens.com
For a free color catalog describing Gareth Stevens Publishing's list
of high-quality books, call 1-800-542-2595 (USA) or 1-800-387-3178 (Canada).
Gareth Stevens Publishing's fax: 1-877-542-2596

Library of Congress Cataloging-in-Publication Data

Burstein, John.
    Rabbits / John Burstein.
      p. cm. — (Slim Goodbody's inside guide to pets)
    Includes bibliographical references and index.
    ISBN-10: 0-8368-8958-4   ISBN-13: 978-0-8368-8958-1 (lib. bdg.)
    1. Rabbits—Juvenile literature. I. Title.
  SF453.2.B86 2008
  636.932'2—dc22   2007033460

This edition first published in 2008 by
Gareth Stevens Publishing
A Weekly Reader® Company
1 Reader's Digest Road
Pleasantville, NY 10570-7000 USA

Photos: All photos from iStock Photos except p. 8 (top) courtesy of www.skullsunlimited.com
Illustrations: Ben McGinnis, Adventure Advertising
Thanks to Susanne Whitaker, Reference/Collection Development Librarian, Flower-Sprecher Veterinary
Library, Cornell University, for help in researching images

Managing Editor: Valerie J. Weber, Wordsmith Ink
Designer: Tammy West, Westgraphix LLC
Gareth Stevens Senior Managing Editor: Lisa M. Guidone
Gareth Stevens Creative Director: Lisa Donovan

Printed in the United States of America

1 2 3 4 5 6 7 8 9 10 10 09 08

CONTENTS

Words that appear in the glossary are printed in **boldface** type the first time they occur in the text.

HOP RIGHT IN

Hello! My name is Rosie. I'm here to tell you about the cutest, sweetest pets in the world — rabbits. We have big eyes, huge ears, wiggly noses, strong back legs, and adorable tails.

I live indoors with my owner. Long ago, however, all rabbits lived in the wild. For example, rabbits were reported in Spain three thousand years ago. As a matter of fact, **Phoenician** sailors long ago once called Spain "the land of the rabbit."

Almost two thousand years ago, Romans in Italy and Africa started raising rabbits in cages and pens. About fifteen hundred years ago, we were brought to other countries, such as France and England. In those days, rabbits were raised as a source of food and fur. Thank goodness, things have changed. Now my owner wants to pet me, not eat me!

Today, pet rabbits can be found in homes all over the world. There are rabbits in India, Japan, Europe, Russia, China, Australia, and the United States.

Russia

England

EUROPE

France

Italy

Spain

China

Japan

United States

India

AFRICA

AUSTRALIA

My Life So Far

I guess I should tell you a few things about myself.

I am three years old. I spend a lot of my day sleeping and eating. I enjoy being around my owner, and I even like the family cat (sometimes).

Rosie Reports

Housing your rabbit indoors is the best way for your family and pet to get to know each other. Rabbits should also have plenty of time outside of their cages to play with your family.

Wolves, foxes, bobcats, weasels, hawks, eagles, owls, and others are always looking for a tasty meal. If wild rabbits are not alert enough, smart enough, or quick enough, they can end up as somebody's dinner.

Rabbits may not be good fighters, but we are great runners. We know how to keep quiet, and we are terrific at building hiding places. In the wild, rabbits hide underground in **warrens**. Warrens are made up of tunnels that connect rooms together. They can be up to 9 feet (2.7 meters) underground.

Still a Little Wild

You may think that pet rabbits and wild rabbits are very different. Wrong! For thousands of years, rabbits have faced a dangerous world. The lessons we learned over time stick with us.

Pet rabbits may live with people who protect us, but we never really let down our guard. If I am scared, I will run away just like a wild rabbit. I may not burrow underground, but I do have a hiding place. It is inside my hutch, a special rabbit house that my owner bought. As you will see in my book, a rabbit's bones, muscles, **organs**, and senses are all designed to keep us safe.

Rosie Reports

Rabbits need a lot of room to move around, so be sure your rabbit's cage is big enough. His cage should be at least five times his size, so he can stretch out completely. He should also be able to stand up on his hind legs without bumping his head on the top of the cage. If you use a wire cage, put a layer of cardboard on the floor. Rabbits have soft feet.

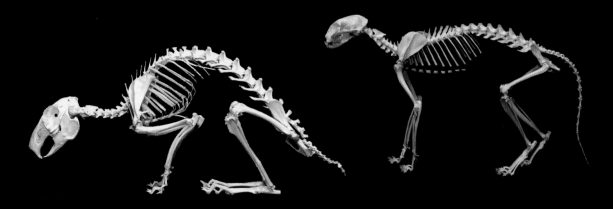

RABBIT SKELETON

CAT SKELETON

My skeleton is lighter than the skeleton of other animals my size.

A 10-pound (4.5-kilogram) rabbit has a skeleton that weighs about 12 ounces (.3 kg). A 10-pound cat has a skeleton that weighs about 21 ounces (.6 kg). A lighter skeleton means less body weight to move when running away from an enemy.

My spine has a beautiful curved shape. It ends in a few short tailbones.

Cats' and dogs' four legs are all the same length. I'm different. My back legs are a lot longer than my front legs.

FUN FACT

If I do not have enough time to run, I may try to trick my enemy by not moving at all. I stay as still as a statue and hope that I am not seen.

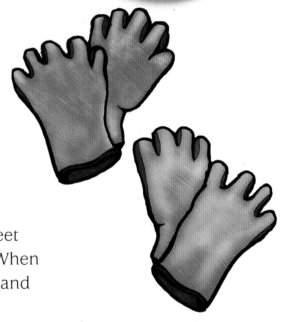

Staying on My Toes

If I had to buy gloves for my feet, I would need two sets that did not match. (Luckily, I do not need gloves. I have lots of fur to keep me warm.) I have five toes on my front feet and only four toes on my back feet. When I move, I travel on the tips of my toes and not on flat feet the way humans do.

Rosie Reports

Rabbit bones can break easily. If you lift your rabbit up, please do it with great care. Always pick her up by placing one hand under her chest. Use your other hand to hold her rear feet. Keep her close to your chest, and do not let her have anything to kick against. You can wrap a towel or blanket around her to keep her snug. Be careful because she may struggle to get away.

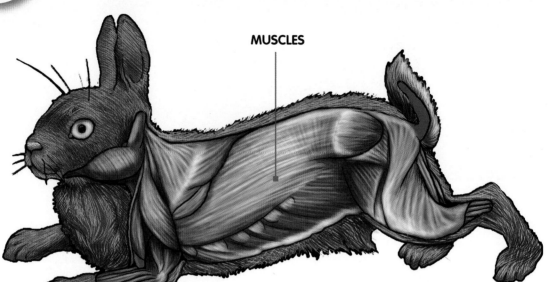

MUSCLES

I have really strong leg muscles. If an enemy is after me, I can run like the wind. I can speed along at close to 35 miles (56 kilometers) an hour. As I run, I zigzag back and forth. This movement tricks my enemy, so it cannot catch me.

I can also jump really high, leaping over things in my path. If I am being chased, I can hop straight up in the air, twist around, and land facing a totally different direction. A friend of mine once jumped 9 feet (2.7 m) to escape a fox.

If I am caught, my back legs can give some powerful kicks. I can also box a little with my front legs if I have to. Once in a while, I will even bite, using my teeth and strong jaw muscles.

A Warning Tail

If I sense danger and have enough time, I thump the ground hard before running away. This noise sends a warning to other nearby rabbits. As I run, I raise my tail like a flag to frighten my enemy and warn others.

Rosie Reports
Your pet rabbit needs exercise to stay healthy. Please give him time to run around outside his cage every day.

CHOMP AND CHEW

My teeth never, ever stop growing. My front teeth grow about 5 inches (13 centimeters) each year. My cheek teeth grow about 3 to 4 inches (8 to 10 cm) per year.

I bet you're wondering how teeth that keep growing can still fit in my mouth. The answer is simple. I keep wearing my teeth down by gnawing and chewing on stuff. For example, I gnaw on sticks, blocks of wood, roots, and chew toys. If you don't watch out, I may even chomp on your birthday present!

If I do not get enough things to chew, my teeth can grow too long. If they do, I must go to the **vet** to have them trimmed.

FUN FACT
Rabbits get two sets of teeth just like humans do. We lose our first set before we are born or right afterward. Then our second set grows in . . . and in . . . and . . . in!

Smile!

When I smile in the mirror, I can count twenty-eight nice, white teeth. An adult human has thirty-two teeth. My front teeth on the top and bottom are called incisors. I use my incisors to cut food into small pieces. Then I pass the food back to my cheek teeth, which are called premolars and molars. These teeth grind the food down.

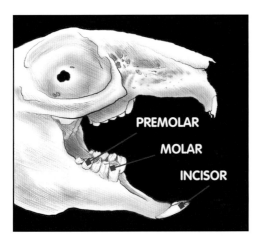

PREMOLAR

MOLAR

INCISOR

HUMAN TEETH

I hope you won't be upset, but I think you look a little funny when you eat. Your jaw moves up and down when you chew, instead of sideways like my jaw does.

Rosie Reports

Be careful about what you give your rabbits to gnaw on. For example, the branches of apricot, cherry, peach, plum, and redwood trees are poisonous. Because rabbits like to chew, make sure that all electrical cords in your house are out of their reach.

DOUBLE DIGESTION

Rabbits do not eat any meat. We must get all our energy from grasses and other plants and food pellets. These foods can be tough and hard to **digest**. When we eat these foods, we only get about half the **nutrients** that we need to stay healthy. To get the rest of the nutrients, we poop the food out in soft clumps and then eat those clumps. In other words, the food passes through two times. The second time gives us the rest of the nutrients that we need.

It may sound a little disgusting to you, but I think of it as a way to recycle my food. Double **digestion** helps me get the most nutrition from the food I eat.

SOFT CLUMPS

POOP

Rosie Reports

Your rabbit's **digestive system** is very sensitive. You shouldn't feed her some foods, including chocolate, cookies, crackers, cereals, bread, pasta, salty or sugary snacks, nuts, or corn. These foods will make your rabbit sick.

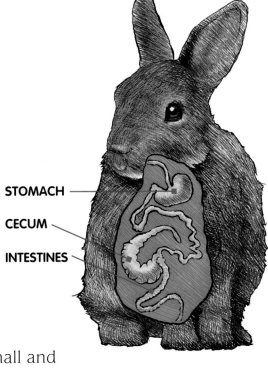

STOMACH

CECUM

INTESTINES

My Cecum, Your Appendix

After I swallow the clumps, they go to an organ called the cecum. Part of my **intestines**, the cecum is very large. It can hold ten times more food than my stomach can. Humans have a cecum too, but it is small and unused. You have another name for it — the appendix.

After food is digested a second time in the cecum, I poop it out again. This poop is hard and round. You'll be glad to know that we do not eat the second kind of poop. Since a lot of the food I eat is dry, I need to drink lots of fresh water everyday. If I don't get enough water, I will eat less and less. After three days without water, I will pretty much stop eating.

I am one of the hairiest pets you could own. I am almost completely covered with hair. The tip of my nose doesn't have hair, though. I even have tough hair on the bottom of my feet instead of footpads like dogs and cats.

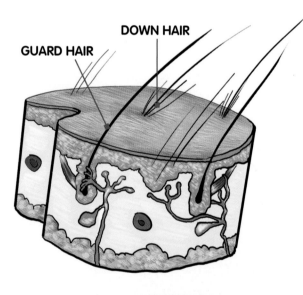

GUARD HAIR

DOWN HAIR

I have two kinds of hair. My thick coat of short, soft hairs close to my skin is called down. It helps keep me warm. My second coat is made of longer hairs called guard hairs. They protect my down hairs.

FUN FACT

Female rabbits have a large fold of skin under their chin called a dewlap. They pull out hair from their dewlap and use it to line nests for their babies.

No Barber for Me, Thanks!

With all of this hair, you might think I would need a lot of haircuts. Nope! I never need a haircut for one simple reason. One to four times a year, all my old hair falls out, and new hair grows in! This process is called molting.

Luckily, molting does not happen everywhere at once, or I would be totally bald for part of the year! First I start losing the hair on my head, then the hair on my neck, then on my back, stomach, and on to the end of my body. Sometimes rabbits lose their hair differently. I have a bunny buddy who loses his hair in patches all over his body.

Another name for rabbit hair is fur. Fur comes in lots of colors and lengths. Fur can be long, short, or in between. Its color can be brown, gray, white, or mixed.

Rosie Reports
Brush your rabbit often to get rid of loose hair. When he is molting, brush him every day. If you don't, he may swallow it when he cleans himself. Remember, he can't vomit up hairballs like a cat does. The dead hair can make him sick. He might need surgery to get it out.

Lots of animals have whiskers, including cats, dogs, and mice. I have lots of whiskers too. They grow near my mouth, on my nose and cheeks, and above my eyes.

My whiskers are long, strong, stiff hairs that grow out from my skin. The base of each whisker is attached to **nerves** in my skin. When my whiskers brush against something, they move. This movement causes the nerves to send a message to my brain.

By the Width of My Whiskers

My whiskers are as long as my body is wide. This width helps me get around in the dark. If my whiskers don't touch the sides of an opening, I know that it's wide enough to slip through. In the wild, whiskers are useful when rabbits are in dark, narrow places such as warrens. They also help rabbits find their way safely at night.

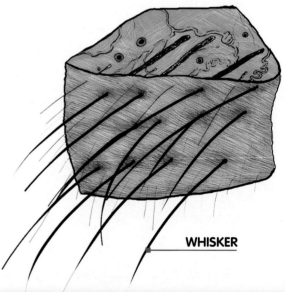

WHISKER

Rosie Reports

Never trim your rabbit's whiskers. She will not be able to get around as well. She might even get stuck in a hole that is too small!

Suppose you woke up in the middle of the night. Suppose all the lights were out, and it was pitch-black. Imagine that you wanted to move around your room. Since your eyes couldn't help you, what would you do? I bet you would hold your hands out in front of you and feel your way along. That plan won't work for me because I need my front feet to walk. My whiskers sure come in handy here.

Since humans don't have whiskers, it may be hard for you to really understand how helpful they are. Here's an experiment to try. Close your eyes and have a friend blow a very soft breath on your eyelashes. Your eyelashes will move a tiny bit in the breeze. This movement lets you know your friend is right next to you, even though you don't see him or her.

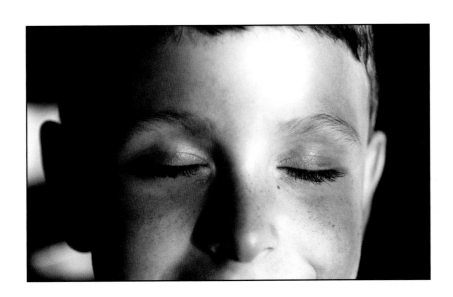

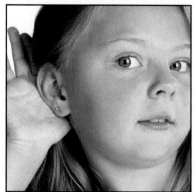

My ears are longer than yours. They are more than 2 inches (5 cm) long. Long ears let me hear more sound. The more sound I hear, the better I can protect myself from possible danger.

Hearing is my most important sense. I depend on hearing more than sight. I might not be able to see a dangerous hidden animal, but I can hear it. I can even hear soft sounds that come from far away. If an animal is sneaking up on me, my terrific sense of hearing gives me the chance to escape.

Cool Ears

Some people can wiggle their ears. That is no trick for a rabbit. I can move my ears forward and backward. I can even move my ears separately and hear sounds coming from two different directions at the same time.

My ears do another important job. When I get hot, my ears release heat into the air, keeping me cool. My ears are like natural air conditioners!

Rosie Reports

A rabbit's ears are delicate. They can be hurt easily. Never lift a rabbit up or hold him by his ears. Clean your rabbit's ears every two weeks to remove any dirt or wax that has built up. Use a cotton swab and don't go deeper into the ear than where you can see clearly.

21

EYES SEE YOU

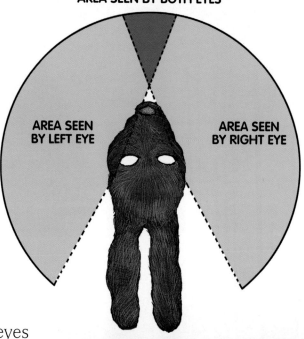

AREA SEEN BY BOTH EYES

AREA SEEN
BY LEFT EYE

AREA SEEN
BY RIGHT EYE

I have large, round eyes set wide apart. One eye looks out to my right side, and the other looks out to my left side. The position of my eyes gives me a wide range of vision. I can see what is going on all around me.

I can spot enemies who might be creeping up from the side, from behind, and from above. I can even see two things at the same time, for example, an enemy and a path of escape.

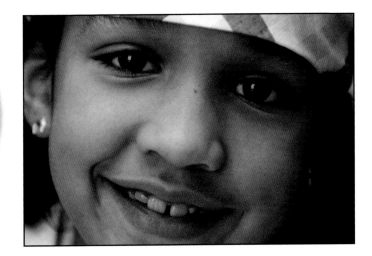

FUN FACT

I can see about eight times better than you can when the light is dim, for example, at sunrise and sunset.

Humans can't do this. They mostly see what is right in front of them and just a little of what is on either side of them.

My eyes are also good at spotting motion. If something is moving, even far away, I can usually see it. I do not have good close-up vision, however. I must rely on my senses of smell and touch to help me know what is nearby.

I do have a blind spot, however. I can't see what is right below my mouth. I must use my lips and whiskers to help me find food.

Rosie Reports

The next time you reach into your rabbit's cage or hutch, do not move your hand toward his blind spot. A hand coming straight at that area can really scare him.

23

My nose may be a lot smaller than yours, but my sense of smell is much better than yours. I don't like to brag, but when it comes to sniffing odors, I am a real champ. I have about 100 million smell-receiving nerves in my nose. Humans only have 5 or 6 million.

A rabbit's nose is always twitching — back and forth and up and down. I twitch about 20 to 120 times per minute. This movement is called nose blinking. It helps me identify different odors and find food. As I wiggle my nose and pull in air, I part the split in my upper lip. This action improves my ability to pick up scents.

Even when I am sleeping, my nose keeps twitching. I never stop checking the air for smells that mean danger. I do not want an enemy sneaking up on me. The only time my nose stops twitching is when I am completely relaxed.

FUN FACT

I can also leave an odor when I want to. When I leave my scent, other rabbits know that I live nearby. I release my scent through scent **glands**. One of them is on the underside of my chin.

Taste

I have a big, strong tongue and a great sense of taste. **Taste buds** on my tongue connect to nerves. These nerves send information to my brain about sweet, sour, bitter, and salty flavors.

All together I have about seventeen thousand taste buds in my mouth. Some are in my tongue, and some are in my throat. You have about ten thousand taste buds. Most of yours are on your tongue.

Rosie Reports

Pet rabbits can't tell which plants are dangerous to taste. Be sure to remove harmful plants from places your rabbit can reach. Some plants that are poisonous for rabbits are buttercups, bluebells, carnations, daffodils, holly, ivy, mistletoe, oleander, and onions.

Sometimes people confuse me with one of my relatives — the hare. Since this is a pretty common mistake, I want to set the record straight. Rabbits and hares are not the same. Hares usually have longer ears, run faster, and weigh more than rabbits. There are lots of other differences too. For example:

- Rabbit babies are born naked and blind. They start to see about ten days after birth.

- Hares are born with fur, and they can see right away. In fact, hares can live on their own about one hour after they are born.

- Rabbits need a few weeks before they are able to run.

- Hares are able to run a few minutes after birth.

- Wild rabbits live together in groups in large underground warrens.

- Wild hares build simple nests and usually live alone or in very small groups.

FUN FACT
In the wild, as many as twenty rabbits live together in warrens.

- A baby rabbit is called a kitten.

- A baby hare is called a leveret.

- A rabbit's fur remains the same color all year-round.

- A hare's fur changes color from grayish brown in summer to white in winter.

- Rabbits are an average length of 15¾ inches (40 cm).

- Hares are an average length of 21½ inches (55 cm).

Rosie Reports

The more you know about your rabbit, the more you can do to keep her happy and healthy. I'm glad I was able to tell you a few things about us, but there is a lot more information available. For example, your pet storeowner can probably answer many questions. You can visit your local library for more rabbit books. Finally, I think it's a good idea to talk with other rabbit owners. You might even go for a visit and bring your rabbit along for a play date!

AMAZING FACTS

I hope you have enjoyed reading my book. I wish I could tell you more about us, but I can hear my owner coming with some tasty radishes. While I'm gnawing on my treat, you can read these amazing rabbit facts.

- Most rabbits live five to seven years. The longest-lived rabbit was nearly nineteen years old when he died.

- The world's biggest rabbit weighs more than 23 pounds (10.4 kg). It is bigger than most two-year-old children.

- The smallest rabbit is less than 8 inches long (20 cm) and weighs less than .1 pounds (0.4 kg).

- Female rabbits can have up to thirty-eight babies each year.

- Newborn babies start to eat solid food at sixteen days old.

- Adult male rabbits are called bucks, and females are called does.

- Rabbits can **communicate** their feelings in certain ways. We can tell you that we feel happy with soft, purring sounds. We will also softly click or quietly grind our teeth. If we are angry, we may grunt, growl, or grind our teeth loudly.

- The longest rabbit ears on record measured more than 31 inches (79 cm) long.

- Rabbit eyes come in several colors, including pink.

- Rabbits have a third eyelid that helps protect their eyes.

- Rabbits clean themselves top to bottom five times a day!

- Rabbits' lower teeth grow faster than their upper teeth.

- The world record for the rabbit high jump is 3.28 feet (1 m).

- The world record for the longest rabbit jump is over 9 feet (3 m)!

- As far as we know, the largest number of baby rabbits in a litter is twenty-four. It has happened twice — once in 1978 and again in 1999.

- The smallest wild rabbit breed in North America is the pygmy or little Idaho rabbit, which weighs slightly less than 1 pound (.45 kg).

- There are over 150 different rabbit coat colors but only 5 eye colors — brown, blue, blue-grey, marbled, and pink.

GLOSSARY

breeds — different groups of rabbits that share the same features

communicate — to pass information along so others understand the meaning

digest — to break down food and change it into energy that the body needs to work

digestion — the process of breaking food down into nutrients needed by the body

digestive system — the group of organs, including the stomach and the intestines, that breaks down food and changes it into energy that the body needs

glands — parts of the body that make special chemicals needed for the body to work properly

intestines — parts of the body through which food passes after it is eaten and leaves the stomach

nerves — special cells that join together and carry signals to and from the brain

nutrients — things needed by people, animals, and plants to live and grow

organs — parts of the body, such as the heart, lungs, stomach, or liver, that do a specific job

Phoenician — describes a person from ancient Phoenicia, the area that is now Syria and Lebanon

taste buds — groups of cells located in the mouth or throat that form tiny bumps and are connected to nerves that send taste information to the brain

vet — short for *veterinarian*, a doctor who takes care of animals

warrens — series of connected underground tunnels where rabbits live together

FOR MORE INFORMATION

BOOKS

101 Facts about Rabbits. 101 Facts about Pets (series). Julia Barnes (Gareth Stevens)

Pet Rabbits. Pet Pals (series). Julia Barnes (Gareth Stevens)

Rabbit. ASPCA Pet Care Guides for Kids (series). Mark Evans (DK Publishing)

Rabbit. Ting Morris (Smart Apple Media)

Rabbits. Keeping Pets (series). Louise A. Spilsbury (Heinemann)

Rabbits, Pikas, and Hares. Animals in Order Series. Sara Swan Miller (Scholastic Library Publishing)

WEB SITES

ASPCA Animaland Pet Care
www.aspca.org/site/PageServer?pagename = kids_pc_rabbit_411
Find out basic facts about rabbits and how to care for them. You can also click on a link to watch Pet Care Cartoons.

Fact Monster: Pets
factmonster.info/pets.html
Scroll down to find articles on rabbits on this site, which has information about many kinds of pets.

House Rabbit Society
www.rabbit.org
Click on the links on this international nonprofit group's Web site to learn about rabbit care, behavior, health, and more.

Your Pet Rabbit
www.bbc.co.uk/cbbc/wild/pets/rabbit.shtml
Check out this interactive site to learn loads about your rabbit and its behavior.

Publisher's note to educators and parents: Our editors have carefully reviewed these Web sites to ensure that they are suitable for children. Many Web sites change frequently, however, and we cannot guarantee that a site's future contents will continue to meet our high standards of quality and educational value. Be advised that children should be closely supervised whenever they access the Internet.

ABOUT THE AUTHOR

John Burstein (also known as Slim Goodbody) has been entertaining and educating children for over thirty years. His programs have been broadcast on CBS, PBS, Nickelodeon, USA, and Discovery. He has won numerous awards including the Parent's Choice Award and the President's Council's Fitness Leader Award. Currently, Mr. Burstein tours the country with his multimedia live show "Bodyology." For more information, please visit slimgoodbody.com.